MRITYUNJAYA

Deepa Raghavan

Chennai • Bangalore

CLEVER FOX PUBLISHING
Chennai, India

Published by CLEVER FOX PUBLISHING 2023
Copyright © Deepa Raghavan 2023

All Rights Reserved.
ISBN: 978-93-56480-22-3

This book has been published with all reasonable efforts taken to make the material error-free after the consent of the author. No part of this book shall be used, reproduced in any manner whatsoever without written permission from the author, except in the case of brief quotations embodied in critical articles and reviews.

The Author of this book is solely responsible and liable for its content including but not limited to the views, representations, descriptions, statements, information, opinions and references ["Content"]. The Content of this book shall not constitute or be construed or deemed to reflect the opinion or expression of the Publisher or Editor. Neither the Publisher nor Editor endorse or approve the Content of this book or guarantee the reliability, accuracy or completeness of the Content published herein and do not make any representations or warranties of any kind, express or implied, including but not limited to the implied warranties of merchantability, fitness for a particular purpose. The Publisher and Editor shall not be liable whatsoever for any errors, omissions, whether such errors or omissions result from negligence, accident, or any other cause or claims for loss or damages of any kind, including without limitation, indirect or consequential loss or damage arising out of use, inability to use, or about the reliability, accuracy or sufficiency of the information contained in this book.

Dedication

To every daughter who is the epitome of courage, love, confidence and dedication.

ACKNOWLEDGEMENT

I would like to thank my FAMILY
for their continuous love and support.

THE RESTING PLACE

The afternoon sun rays fall sharply on the crowd of people standing close to one another. As the pyre is lit, a few of them are weeping, some standing still with no reaction and some trying to wipe off the sweat from their brow. A few others are hugging and consoling a 25-year-old man who has just lit the pyre with his bare hands. He lets out an emotional scream, "*Maai, Maai.*" An elderly person standing next to him wraps him in his arms and consoles him. He calms down and is now staring blankly at the burning pyre. There is pin-drop silence, and even the crackle of the flame is heard distinctly. A man pours more *ghee* into the pyre to help it burn better. The flames rise higher with the addition of the flammable liquid. The man pouring the *ghee* is around 40 years old, medium built, and slightly stout. His tanned and weather-beaten face makes him look older than his age. He is dressed in a creased and soiled dhoti paired with a short kurta. He takes a stave (a bamboo fire poker) and pokes it into the burning logs, proving that he is an expert in his job. He is Babasaheb, the in-charge, the one who owns and manages the only *Smashaan Bhoomi* (crematorium) in Kurni village of Kagal Taluka in Kolhapur district. Everyone addresses him as Baba, the actual meaning of being a father in Marathi!

He looks here and there and shouts, "Madhav, Madhav." An 11-year-old boy is sitting a little away, with a twig in his hand, trying to draw something on mud. He didn't care about his name being called. Baba again calls out to Madhav. Without picking his head, he replies, "Baba, can't you see I am busy."

The villagers look at Baba, who then runs towards the boy and very softly tells him, "You are my darling son, aren't you? Why do you answer back and that too in front of all these people?" Madhav turns a deaf ear. Baba immediately removes a one-rupee coin from his kurta pocket and gives it to Madhav. Madhav's eyes light up. Baba smiles at him and says, "In the evening, you can have your favourite sweet from the nearby sweet vendor, happy?"

Madhav gets up, pats the mud from his short pants, looks Baba in the face, and asks "You want me to go and get some more wooden logs, right?" Baba smiles at him, and before he can acknowledge it, Madhav sprints towards the other end of the ground where there is a shanty to keep all the material required for cremation. Next to this shanty is a hut with a thatched roof. Standing by the door of this hut is an 11-year-old girl. She is Baba's daughter and Madhav's twin sister, Jaya.

She wears a curious look on her face as she sees the flames from the pyre reach up the sky. Madhav looks at her and says, "Jaya, go in. What are you doing here?" She is still focused on seeing what all Baba is doing there. Madhav picks a few heavy logs on his head and walks back when he trips and falls. Jaya immediately rushes toward him. "Should I help you with these?" she asks. Madhav gets up, gives her an angry look, and reiterates, "Didn't you hear me the first time? Don't stand here; just go in, else I will tell Baba."

Jaya moves back; she wants to say something when Madhav asks authoritatively "Have you done my homework?" Jaya is silent. He tells her sternly, "You better finish it, else I will tell Baba that you are interested in helping with these funeral rituals, and if he gets angry, don't say that I didn't warn you."

Jaya runs into the thatched hut, not looking back even once. Madhav smirks as he carries the logs on his head and goes towards Baba. He feels proud of himself as he is aware that his father's job is different from other people in the village, who are primarily farmers or labourers. Madhav shows off in front of his school friends because he thinks he is fearless, whereas most of his friends fear coming to the crematorium or are discouraged by their parents even to discuss death or funerals. So, Madhav throws his weight around not only in school but also at home.

Inside the hut, Jaya is completing Madhav's homework. Jaya's mother, Sakubai, a 30-something lady, is sitting and kneading dough to make *Bhakri* (a typical Maharashtrian flatbread) by the other corner of the hut. She is watching Jaya from the corner of her eye while kneading the dough. Jaya is writing but is also mumbling something to herself. Sakubai questions her, "Jaya, what are you talking to yourself? Speak loudly so that I can also hear you?

Jaya gathers courage and speaks up, "*Aai*, tell me one thing. Why is Madhav allowed to do all the work and why am I always reminded that I am a girl and I need to stay indoors?"

Sakubai corrects her, "You can also work; who has stopped you." Jaya has a glee on her face; she gets up to leave the hut when Sakubai adds, "But you can work here with me. Help me make this *Bhakri*; I'll teach you how to make tasty *Bhakri*, so that when you get married, you can feed your family and make them happy."

Jaya angrily replies, "No *Aai*, I want to do some other work, not being a housewife or cook." Sakubai snaps at her, "Lower your volume. If your Baba hears you, he will get angry not only at you but also at me. Come here, give me a helping hand." Jaya nods her head and vents, "I have to finish Madhav's homework because he is doing other important work. This is not right *Aai*." Sakubai has a dejected expression as she retorts, "God, please give her little wisdom." Jaya looks blankly at the book realising that her voice will never be heard in this house.

Baba and Madhav come to the hut after all the villagers have left. The pyre is still burning. The flames are not burning violently and have died down. Sakubai immediately keeps their food ready.

She instructs Jaya to give them water to drink. Jaya reluctantly helps. Sakubai calls Madhav, makes him sit next to her, and affectionately runs her fingers through his hair, which he detests and moves away. She smiles, starts feeding him *Bhakri,* and exclaims, "My loving child, you must be exhausted today. Let me press your legs after you finish lunch, and then you take some rest, is that fine?

Jaya immediately reacts, "Who will do his homework then? Let the teacher punish him tomorrow."

Madhav counters, "For all you know, I may be busy tomorrow also, not like you having nothing to do. You better finish my homework; that way, you will be able to learn the same thing twice."

Sakubai smiles and says her son *is smart.*

Baba is sitting quietly and eating his *Bhakri.* Once Baba and Madhav have finished lunch, Sakubai and Jaya sit to eat food. Jaya is unhappy with all these age-old traditions where the woman is given second-hand treatment. Jaya helps clean up everything. Baba and Madhav are resting. Jaya goes back to her books when she hears "*Ram Naam Satya hai*"(commonly chanted by *Hindus* while carrying a dead body to be cremated) repeatedly.

She runs to the door to see a crowd of people entering the crematorium. Another funeral service to be rendered, she thinks; she rushes back and wakes up Baba. He immediately gets up, washes his face, and instructs Jaya to wake Madhav up. Jaya tries waking him up, but he is sleeping like a log. She gathers courage, goes up to Baba, who is on his way out, and says, "Baba." She takes a deep breath before muttering, "Baba, since Madhav is not getting up, can I come and help you?" Baba gives her a stern look; without uttering a word, he yells, "Saku, Saku wake up Madhav fast, tell him to come and help me and also drive some sense into your girl. You have not taught her what she needs to say and when."

He leaves, Jaya is heartbroken, and before she can assimilate what Baba said, Sakubai screams, "Don't you realise how over-worked your Baba is. Why do you harass him with your silly questions? Don't you understand that you are not supposed to be doing certain kinds of work, but you won't listen? I think we made a big mistake by sending you to school. I have heard people say that once a girl is educated, she gets out of hand and acts over smart. I think I should stop your schooling."

Her mother's anger pierces her heart, and she pleads with tears in her eyes, "No, *Aai,* I won't trouble Baba or you again, but please don't stop my schooling. Please, I beg of you *Aai*, please."

Sakubai stands there unmoved as Jaya falls at her feet, begging. "Go, go and wake up, Madhav, hurry up." Jaya wipes her tears and takes extra effort to wake Madhav, who doesn't want to budge. Sakubai has to coax him to get up by giving him a rupee, but he doesn't give in. Sakubai successfully wakes him only when she gives him an extra rupee. The barter system has been the way of life for Madhav, and he gets money for the services he renders to help Baba in the crematorium. He moves out lazily towards the crematorium, Sakubai is finishing the household errands, and Jaya cries behind her books.

RANI OF KURNI

*T*ime slips by, and seeing dead bodies, funerals, and mourners is a regular feature in Jaya and Madhav's life. For people coming to burn their loved ones, it is an earth-shattering affair, but for them, it is a daily chore. They are unmoved by the entire process. Jaya no longer insists on helping Baba. Even though she is not allowed to help Baba, she has been a silent spectator for all these years. Being a quick learner and a keen observer, her mind has registered all the activities done by Baba.

Jaya is dedicated not only to her studies but also to helping *Aai* with household chores. Madhav continues to be a truant by bunking school and neglecting the work given by Baba. He still gets away because of Sakubai's support and pampering. A helpless Baba doesn't pay much heed and is only concerned with his job being done.

School is Jaya's happy place, and the last two years have been exceptionally exciting, thanks to a new teacher joining the school. Mughda, the new teacher, who joined the school two years back, has been instrumental in bringing about a rapid change. She is the only lady teacher in the school and has a friendly approach from day one toward all the students, especially the female students. Jaya idolises Mughda, who is self-made and committed to bringing about a change in what people think about a girl child.

Mughda was born in a Chiklap village in the Raigarh district. Her parents were poor farmers who used to work on other people's land to make a living. Her school was located far away, and she walked more than four kilometres to and fro daily. She used to leave her home at 5:00 am to reach her school on time. One of the hardest challenges she encountered was poverty, but her parents encouraged her to study. She still remembers how her parents suffered but never let her miss a meal. All this empowered her to strive better and achieve more. She was able to fulfil her dreams thanks to the support from the NGO, *Mann Ki Udaan*, whose representatives had visited her village.

They aimed to educate the girl child, train women, and help them sharpen their skills. Free education for an aspiring village girl like Mughda was a dream come true. She grabbed the opportunity, and there was no looking back. She excelled in everything she did and passed with flying colours. Once she completed her education, she went ahead to do B.Ed. (Teacher's Training course). The NGO had given her a new lease of life, and she too wanted to be instrumental in making a difference in many lives, especially that of a girl child.

On weekends and holidays, Mughda ensures that she visits the houses in the village to encourage parents to send their daughters to school. She enforces the program of *'Betiyon ki pragati, Desh ki unnati!'* (Daughters will progress, the country will develop*)*

She regularly shares inspiring stories of female leaders like Ahilyabai Holkar, Savitribai Phule, and Indira Gandhi. All these stories fascinate Jaya, and she believes that one day she too will achieve something and make her parents proud. She tries sharing these stories with *Aai,* who keeps discouraging her, "You will not gain anything from all this. One day you have to get married and manage your house." A dejected 13-year-old no more debates with her *Aai*; she knows it is futile, so she keeps to herself.

She participates in all the activities at school and is constantly encouraged by Mughda. She tops the class and is an all-rounder. Her teacher keeps motivating her because she sees a splitting image of herself in Jaya. She believes that Jaya is extraordinary and will surely make a mark wherever she goes. They both share a special bond.

Under the leadership and guidance of Mughda, the school now participates in many inter-school competitions, something the school hasn't heard of before. Intelligent students like Jaya and a few others are happy to get this kind of exposure, but there are exceptions like Madhav, who feel it is a waste of time and prefer bunking school.

Jaya and the other students eagerly look forward to the next inter-school poetry competition. For the first time, such a competition was to be hosted in their school. The staff and students are delighted to decorate the school and create a wonderful ambiance for all the participants. Jaya is nominated to represent the school in the competition. She has mixed feelings; she is overwhelmed and tense as she does not want to let her teachers or school down.

Jaya and Madhav are walking back home from school. She is silent and lost in her thoughts. Madhav mocks her, "Now you won't talk because you feel you are the most important person in this school. Do you think you can win? Is it that easy? There will be so many schools and many participants. You may not be able to face the crowd or utter a word in front of them. You may just freeze; you better withdraw your name from this competition. Don't overindulge in all this and make a fool out of yourself and bring shame to the school and us. I don't want to be called the brother of a loser, understand?"

Jaya is distraught. She is unable to control her emotions and starts weeping as she reaches home. *Aai* wants to know what is wrong. Madhav lies through his teeth by saying "Jaya hadn't finished her homework, so the teacher punished her today, someday this girl..." An annoyed Jaya wants to give him a piece of her mind but decides against it because she knows this is her lone battle, and no one will console or understand her. *Aai* isn't moved either and instructs Jaya to finish some chores. Pointing to the unkept kitchen, Madhav remarks," This is what you need to focus on, do you understand?" He walks away; Jaya feels she is stuck in a whirlpool and can never be rescued.

The next day in school, Jaya confesses to Mughda, "Sorry teacher, I think I just got overly excited yesterday; I developed cold feet. I am an ordinary girl who can't compete with anyone. So, I will not be able to represent our school in this competition. Kindly excuse me this time."

Her teacher sits her down, listens to her patiently, and says, "Jaya, if you are not comfortable, I will not force you to participate. Let me narrate a story to you; it may help you gather your thoughts." She narrates the story of Rani Laxmibai and highlights how the Rani single-handedly fought her enemies. She never underestimated what she could do in a man's world, being a woman. She believed in herself and gave her best but did not track back. We all face hardships, but we need to stand strong and follow our hearts. Wait a minute." She takes a book titled *Manikarnika*, from her bag and gives it to Jaya. "Whenever you face a tough situation, remember the Queen of Jhansi and her 'never give up' attitude. If your thoughts do not support your situation, then this book will keep you company and bail you out," she assures.

The confidence given by her teacher, the motivational story, and the book is good enough to instil faith in Jaya, who now believes that winning or losing is secondary, but participation is important. Jaya gives a warm hug to her teacher, keeps the book close to her heart, and heaving a sigh of relief she leaves for home, not realising that this inspirational story and the book will shape her life for many years to come.

As the day of the competition is approaching, Jaya is tense. She is pacing up and down outside her hut, memorizing her poem. There is a pyre burning at the crematorium, and for the first time, she is disinterested in seeing what Baba is doing. Madhav tries his best to discourage her, but she is unmoved by his mannerisms.

It is the day of the competition. The school looks spick and span, and the *Rangoli* (traditional Indian decorative patterns made with ground rice) at the entrance is vibrant and welcoming. Each classroom is beautifully decorated with Marigold flowers. The fragrance of the flowers lingers in the air, adding freshness to the ambiance. Students from multiple schools are seated in the open ground of the school. The chief guest of this function is the newly elected *Panch* (Ward Member), Mr. Satwalekar a 50-year-old well-built, fair-looking man with a thick moustache. He is attired in a pure white cotton dhoti paired with a full-sleeved, crisp shirt, with a bright turban adorning his head. His personality radiates an aura of power and confidence.

After the initial welcoming and exchanging of pleasantries, the competition begins. As predicted by Madhav, each participant is out-doing the other, and they all seem to be fierce competition for Jaya. Madhav has a sarcastic grin on his face, and he looks at Jaya and signals thumbs-down. Jaya is not influenced; she turns away to look at her teacher, who is smiling at her and signalling a thumbs-up. Her name is announced; she is the last participant for the day as she is from the hosting school. Jaya stands still in front of the mic, her heart pounding faster. She has a tingling feeling in her palms, and her throat tightens. She is about to start when there is a screeching sound from the mic. All the children in the audience shut their ears and let out a squeal, Jaya becomes jittery and is fidgeting with the wire of the mic. Madhav's unkind words, "You may not be able to face the crowd or utter a word in front of them. You may just freeze. Don't overindulge and make a fool out of yourself," echo in her head. It was like he had a premonition that everything would work against her.

The peon tries fixing the snag but is unsuccessful. Jaya is asked to perform without the mic. The technical delay makes the students impatient, causing a commotion, and they seem to have lost interest in the event. Mughda tries to control the situation but in vain. She looks at Jaya with empathy. Jaya realises that things are getting out of hand. She closes her eyes and starts reciting the National anthem. In no time, there is pin-drop silence and everyone stands up in respect of her rendition. She ends the National anthem by saying "*Jai Hind*", then requests everyone to sit down so that she can recite her poem. Before the crowd realises anything, she starts reciting renowned poet Subhadra Kumari Chauhan's poem, *Jhansi ki Rani*. Jaya doesn't miss a word; her rousing and fiery rendition draws everyone's attention. Every paragraph she recites reflects her conviction and confidence. As she ends the poem with the line *"Khoob ladi mardani woh to Jhansi wali Rani thi."* (Fought gallantly, she was the Queen of Jhansi), there is huge applause from all the students. Hearing the crowd screaming, "Once more!" Jaya is elated; her eyes well up, and they are looking out for her teacher, who is also clapping loudly for her.

The crowd settles down, and Mr. Satwalekar is invited on stage to do the honours of declaring the winners. He starts announcing the names of the winners in descending order—schools from Nidhori village and Yamage village bag the third and second prizes. Before announcing the name of the first prize winner, he exclaims, "Today, what we witnessed was a clear depiction of courage. Only a brave warrior who believes in oneself can surpass any hurdle without batting an eyelid. That is exactly what our first prize winner portrayed today. The 'never-give-up' attitude just reiterates that our land can still produce great warriors who can stand up and face any situation single-handedly. I proudly announce Jaya as today's winner. I am honoured that Jaya belongs to my village, and she fought gallantly like the Queen of Jhansi !" As Jaya goes up the stage, she gets a standing ovation. Everyone other than Madhav seems to be happy. She bends and touches Mr. Satwalekar's feet as a mark of respect, seeking his blessings. She is handed over the winning trophy and is asked to say something. "I owe all this to my inspiration, my idol, my *guru,* Mughda teacher. She has been the wind beneath my wings; her constant encouragement made me achieve this feat. She is a blessing to me, our school, and our village. Thank you, teacher," saying this she rushes down the stage, runs towards her teacher, and gives her a tight hug, with tears of joy rolling down her cheeks. Her teacher pats her back, wipes her tears, and says, "I'm so proud of you, Jaya. You are no ordinary girl; for me, you are nothing less than *Manikarnika* herself, so I would like to confer you with the title, '**Rani of Kurni!**'

PYRE OF DREAMS

*J*aya is feeling on top of the world. This win has given her a ray of hope that she will be able to achieve whatever she wants.

She is looking out for Madhav in the school playground, but she cannot find him and walks home alone. Her swift stride seems lyrical and displays happiness. The smile on her face depicts her belief in talking to her parents about her further studies and convincing them about her dream of becoming a teacher in the future, but she is unaware of what is in store for her at home.

She reaches home; there is a funeral pyre burning in the ground. Baba doesn't seem to be around. She rushes inside the hut to share the good news with her family. Seeing her, *Aai* turns away, Madhav is standing in the corner fidgeting with a piece of paper, and Baba is eating his lunch. All are silent. An elated Jaya says, "*Aai-Baba*, I'm sure Madhav would have told you both about what happened in school, but I too want to share my happiness and.." before she can say anything, *Aai* interrupts, "You are happy, after all, that you have done in school? Yes, Madhav updated us, but we are shocked; how? Jaya how? How come you turned out to be like this?"

Aai starts sobbing. Jaya is clueless about what *Aai* is saying. "*Aai* why are you upset? What have I done?" She asks. "Don't make me open my mouth, I kept telling your Baba not to send you to school, but he always believed in you. But today, you have brought shame to us; we won't be able to face anyone." *Aai* continues sobbing. Jaya reacts, "I have brought shame to you? I'm confused. What are you talking about?"

"After doing all this, now will you raise your voice? Madhav told us about your song and dance performance, I'm shocked beyond words Jaya. I'm questioning my upbringing, Oh Lord, why didn't I die before hearing all this?" Cries *Aai* loudly.

"Dance and me? Madhav has lied to you both. How dare you, Madhav? What do you get by doing all this? Everyone in school is proud of me and you are poisoning *Aai-Baba*'s mind with all this rubbish. *Aai* you can ask my teacher; she will tell you the truth," retaliates Jaya.

"I don't want to talk to any outsider; I trust my son, and why will he lie about you, Jaya? Don't forget he is your brother, and he is concerned about us and also respects the limits we have set." Tells *Aai* assertively, then looks at Baba and says, "Will you not say anything? Can't you see she is lying; our life is doomed. You wanted to educate your daughter and see what has happened. She is dancing and singing in school; what if she runs away tomorrow to become an actress. We will have to jump into one of the funeral pyres and immolate ourselves." Baba is quiet. Jaya goes to him, "Baba, please, believe me, Madhav is lying. I did not dance in school," she cries.

Madhav butts in, "You didn't do anything? The school gave you this trophy for nothing, right? Lie to Baba that you didn't sing that Jhansi Rani song, just lie; that is what you have been doing, Jaya, duping us."

"Did you sing a song?" asks Baba firmly. "Baba, let me explain," says Jaya. "Do not try my patience Jaya; just say Yes or No," emphasises Baba.

"Baba, I can explain; it is not a song, but" replies Jaya.

"Yes or No," asks Baba sternly.

"Yes," replies Jaya with tears in her eyes.

Baba pours water on the remaining food on his plate, gets up, and leaves the hut. *Aai* follows him. Jaya calls, "Baba, it was just a poem. Please hear me out, believe me." She holds her trophy tight as she plunges to the floor. Madhav retorts sarcastically, "You thought just by reciting a poem you will become a star overnight…impossible! Do not forget you are a girl; if anyone can become a star, it's only me, so don't try to supersede me anywhere, be it school or home. Am I loud and clear *Jhansi ki Flop Rani*!"

Jaya is crying uncontrollably; *Aai* walks in and yells, "Baba is angry because of you; he didn't hear anything I said. You have upset him; he has left without telling us where he is going. If anything happens to him, you will be responsible, and I will never pardon you." Madhav pretends to console *Aai*, "Don't worry *Aai*, I am here to take care of you and Baba. I will also try and drive some sense into Jaya's head." An angry Jaya cries, "You will drive sense into me? And you think

I am going to listen to you? Let me tell the teacher tomorrow, she will punish you."

"Just keep quiet. Baba has left home and you are still bothered about yourself. How will you say anything to your teacher? I'm going to stop your schooling. You dare step a foot out of this house, and you will see my true colours," screams *Aai*.

"The unwanted attention she has got today has poisoned her mind *Aai*; she seems to be in a dream world. Just see how I burst her dream bubble." Saying this, Madhav goes to Jaya and pulls the trophy from her hand. She struggles to hold on to the trophy, but Madhav is successful in snatching it from her. He runs outside the hut with the trophy. Jaya is howling and running behind him, and before she can fathom what is happening, Madhav dashes toward the burning pyre and throws the trophy at it. A helpless Jaya falls to the ground, seeing her prized possession burnt to ashes.

The sun goes down, and Jaya is sitting outside her hut. Her tears have dried up, and her face resembles a withered flower; the vibrant sunflower face has faded by dusk. *Aai* is unbothered by her, preparing dinner and keeping a watch on the main gate waiting for Baba to return.

Madhav comes from outside and says, "I looked for Baba everywhere, could not find him *Aai*; maybe we need to register a police complaint." *Aai* starts weeping, "it is all because of this girl; now we have to go to the police; they will ask us a hundred questions. Lord, please bail us out of this situation; I promise to offer you fifty-one rupees once Madhav's Baba returns home safely."

Madhav interrupts, "You offer whatever you want to your God later; now come with me to register a police complaint before it is too late." *Aai* wipes her tears, makes her saree ok by ironing it with her hand, and pulls the *pallu* (loose end of a sari) over her head. She comes out of the hut with Madhav, and orders Jaya, "I have kept food on the gas fire to cook; keep an eye on it. Pray that we find your Baba, else I don't know what I will do to you, be ready to bear the consequences. Do you understand?"

As Madhav and *Aai* take a few steps, they see Baba coming. *Aai* runs towards him, and asks emotionally, "Where did you go suddenly? You didn't even think once about what would happen to me if you didn't return? I died a million deaths in the last few hours. Our dear son Madhav went around looking for you, and no one had any idea where you were. Say something, where did you go? Why are you so silent?"

Baba doesn't utter a word and walks towards the hut; seeing Jaya sitting outside, he says, "Come inside Jaya. Did you eat anything?" Jaya looks at Baba, gives him a tight hug, and starts crying. "Wipe your tears; you are my good child, aren't you?" asks Baba. Jaya nods her head in affirmation. He tells Sakubai, "serve food for both of us, today, father and daughter will eat together." *Aai* is surprised to hear Baba's tone, and Madhav is livid. "Baba, she made such a blunder today, and you are sweet-talking to her?" questions Madhav. Before he can say anything more, Baba cuts him, "Madhav, go and see if we have enough stock of all the funeral items; else we will need to go to the market to purchase it tomorrow." An agitated Madhav storms out. A disinterested *Aai* serves food to Baba and Jaya. Hearing all this, Jaya feels reassured and believes she still has some hope.

Baba tells Jaya, "I know you are very talented, my child, but we have certain restrictions in our society. Do you ever wonder why I am not a farmer or a labourer, like many others in this village? The reason is that my forefathers have run this crematorium. For generations, we have been dutifully managing the only crematorium in this village. Seeing our sincerity, the Gram Panchayat decided to offer this land to our family to continue to serve the villagers forever. We are indebted to the *Panchayat* (the local governing body of a village), and I need to keep assuring them that I can run this business without any hurdles, the way my forefathers have run it. Do you know why I don't encourage Madhav to go to school? Because he has to run this crematorium going forward, it doesn't matter how educated he is. By default, this is our family business, and we will keep passing it on to the next generation."

Jaya is listening patiently. He adds, "If we bend any rules, then we will have to surrender this land, and we will be outcast. We will have nowhere to go. I don't want to encourage any action which will disappoint the villagers or the *Panchayat*. Jaya, honestly speaking, you have no choice but to accept this situation. If you still feel you want to do what you think is right, you can rebel and get us in trouble. But I am sure you will tread the line and not bring shame to your family."

Aai heaves a sigh of relief hearing Baba speak, and she knows Jaya will never go against her father's wishes.

Jaya looks at Baba, clasps his hand tight, and assures, "Don't worry, Baba, your Jaya will never do anything to bring shame to you or your family. I just have one request; can I continue my schooling till my Tenth standard. Please, Baba." Baba nods his head half-heartedly.

Both of them silently finish dinner. The silence is deafening, similar to the last journey of a dead person. Jaya eating rice resonates with the rice being placed in a dead person's mouth before his pyre is lit. All this symbolises the last rites of Jaya's dreams, with no mourners, no smoke, or a pyre!

CAGED

*J*aya continues going to school, but she is no longer the same girl. She is silent, does not participate in class, nor is she inquisitive about hearing more stories from her teacher. This goes on for a year. Her irregularity in school worries her teacher. She tries questioning Jaya but gets no response, so she calls Madhav hoping to get some insight into Jaya's problem. A disinterested Madhav informs her that Jaya will be married off once she turns sixteen, so her coming to school makes no sense.

Mughda decides to meet Jaya's parents, hoping to make them understand. She reaches the crematorium; the gate is ajar. She calls out to Jaya and Madhav but gets no response. She tries entering the crematorium, when she sees an old man, having a medium build, slightly stout, running towards her, "Please wait Madam. *Namaste* Madam. I'm sorry, you cannot enter the crematorium. Is there a male member in your house who can come and book the funeral service?" he asks. "I don't want to book a funeral service, I am Mughda, Jaya's teacher from the village school, and I have come to meet her parents," she replies.

Baba looks away, then, with folded hands, says, "Madam, I'm Babasaheb, Jaya's father; I have a small request, please don't influence my child." He bends to touch her feet. She moves two steps back, "Please, please, *Kaka* (uncle), don't do this; you are older than me; why are you touching my feet? I just want to assure you that your daughter is extremely talented. She will bring name and fame not only to your family but to this whole village. Trust me."

Before she can say anything more, Baba interrupts, "Please, Madam, let us be the way we are; we don't want to educate our daughter and make her famous. We are dependent on this village and the villagers. Leave us to our fate, I beg of you. Please leave; if any villager sees a lady at the crematorium gate, hell will break loose. Don't make life difficult for us." Saying this, he turns his back and walks into the crematorium. "Please listen to me, *kaka*, I will talk to the *Panch*, please," she begs. Baba doesn't turn but throws his hands in the air, signalling refutation to whatever she says. A dejected Mughda leaves the crematorium, wondering if things will ever progress in small villages or will girls like Jaya have to give up on their dreams. Jaya's absenteeism in school increases after this episode, and even Mughda cannot bail her out of this situation. She doesn't lose hope, and whenever Jaya comes to school, she motivates her and encourages her to help her in school activities until one day when her transfer orders to Yamage village are announced.

The school arranges a farewell for Mughda. Most of the kids in the school get emotional. Jaya's eyes well up; she gives her a tight hug. "I know one day you will do something so remarkable that everyone will applaud you, Jaya; you will always remain in my thoughts, and I hope the best for you always, my child," kissing Jaya's forehead, her teacher blesses her. Jaya doesn't utter a word; tears are rolling down her eyes, and this seems to be the final nail in her coffin.

Three years pass in a flash, and Jaya has turned 16. As decided earlier, her parents stop her schooling completely. She now keeps herself busy by engaging in cooking, cleaning, and helping *Aai* with household chores and errands. When time permits, she reads her old school books and her favourite book on *Jhansi ki Rani*, gifted by her teacher. She also reads articles from the newspaper pieces in which items are wrapped and brought home. Whatever paper is thrown away, she picks each of it to read.

Jaya's parents are busy groom hunting for Jaya, but she doesn't get many alliances, as no one wants the daughter of a crematorium owner to be their daughter-in-law. Even if they agree to make that compromise, the groom's side makes exorbitant dowry demands to accept Jaya.

Time flies quickly, and over the last five years, *Aai's* frustration with having an unmarried daughter at home has increased by leaps and bounds. She keeps nagging Jaya for every small thing and keeps cursing her fate. Jaya is 21 years old, an age beyond the benchmark age for any village girl to stay unmarried. Baba doesn't speak of his frustration, but his receding hairline, dark circles under his eyes, and wrinkled face talk about his sleepless nights and the worry of having an unmarried daughter at home.

Madhav is his usual self, not bothered about anything that is happening. He has taken to smoking *beedi* (a thin cigarette or mini-cigar filled with tobacco flake), and he also drinks occasionally. If Baba questions him about his vices, his only reply is, "I'm so tensed that my sister, Jaya, is not getting married, I want her to get a nice alliance, be happily settled, and you think I'm smoking *beedi* for my happiness, I'm doing all this to relieve my anxiety."

Only *Aai* believes everything he says; she wails her heart out, "My darling son. Do you see how worked up he is for you, Jaya, in childhood, you used to always complain about him. You are blessed to have a brother like him." Jaya knows that all these are white lies. She turns a deaf ear to whatever claims Madhav and *Aai* make.

Other than making these tall claims and being addicted to smoking *beedi*, Madhav wastes a lot of his time talking to his childhood friend Mangesh on the phone. Mangesh happens to work in a hospital in Mumbai. Madhav is elated and happy to hear Mangesh's version of the happenings in the urban side of the world. Mangesh's narration makes his dreams of leading a city life too, but he feels stuck in this village and now detests the job at the crematorium.

Mangesh is an influencer of sorts in Madhav's life. He promises Madhav a job in the city hospital. He confidently claims that a street-smart person like Madhav is cut to live life in a city rather than wasting his time working in the village crematorium. He assures that once Madhav comes to the city, his life will change big time and he wouldn't have to be at the mercy of his father for any money, and he can easily earn a comfortable living, lead a relaxed and happening life with free-flowing alcohol, cigarettes and no one to question him. Madhav is floored by Mangesh's words and starts building castles in the air. The only favour Mangesh wants from him is to fix Jaya's wedding with his distant cousin Tukaram. A self-centred Madhav, who always believes in the barter system, blindly agrees to whatever Mangesh proposes.

At his behest, Madhav tries convincing his parents of Jaya's alliance with Tukaram. Baba is not convinced; he has never met Mangesh or anyone from his family, nor does he remember having interacted with this family ever, so he finds it hard to believe whatever Madhav is trying to tell him, but Madhav manages to blackmail *Aai* emotionally, "Jaya will be twenty-two in less than eight months, we will have no seekers for her, what will we do then, don't you both want to see her happily settled?

Tukaram is a nice person; whatever I have heard about him from Mangesh makes me confident that he will keep Jaya very happy." *Aai* acknowledges everything Madhav says, but Baba is not convinced, "How do you want me to get my daughter married off to a widower who is double her age? I don't think it's right."

Pugnacious Madhav retorts, "Fine, then you keep your daughter at home and take care of her. You always have an issue with any solution I provide for this house. Manage your house, your daughter's life, and this crematorium. Why do you need me? Mangesh keeps calling me to the city, I'm a doting son and brother and want to fulfil my responsibilities, but no, if you still feel this alliance is improper, then fine. Let Jaya stay here forever."

Hearing Madhav's outburst, *Aai* gets teary, "In today's day and age, where will you find a devoted son like Madhav? If he has got the alliance, then it won't be unsuitable for Jaya. If we let this alliance also slip away, we may not have any more proposals. Let us settle for this one." A vulnerable Baba gives in to the pressure and the day arrives when both the families agree to meet. The meeting is arranged in the village temple as Tukaram's mother is not keen on keeping the first meeting at the girl's place. She is orthodox and believes if anything good has to take place, then it should start from a pious environment and not an inauspicious and unfavourable place located inside a crematorium.

Both the families reach the temple on the designated date; Tukaram, a 40-year-old local labourer, frail-looking, dark-skinned, has curly hair with few strands of grey. He is dressed in a trouser and a full-sleeved kurta, a *Gamcha* (a traditional thin, coarse cotton cloth worn around the neck), and a Gandhi topi. He speaks less and lets his mother do all the talking. She makes a few demands to which Madhav agrees immediately; she also insists on a wedding at the earliest *Muhurat* (the most auspicious day as per the traditional calendar).

The priest announces that any day within the next ten days is auspicious; if not, they will have to wait for another six months to get another auspicious date. Madhav insists on having the wedding within two days. He wants to expedite the marriage, to impress Mangesh, who will then accelerate his chances of getting the city job. Jaya is not happy with this decision but succumbs to parental pressure, and before the family realises, Jaya is married off to Tukaram. *Aai*-Baba and Madhav are put to ease.

As a young bride Jaya doesn't expect much out of this marriage, but she hopes her husband is caring and understanding. Tukaram is a man of few words; he hardly interacts with her, and even if he does, he talks in monosyllables. He is most of the time busy at work, trying to make ends meet. Jaya's mother-in-law calls the shots and keeps ordering her to do multiple things. Jaya realises that nothing has changed in her life, except the location and people around her. She still is a caged bird who has no choice other than staying captive and fulfilling her duties of being a good wife, daughter-in-law, and homemaker.

It is three months since they are married, and Jaya is adjusting, accepting, and taking things in her stride. Tukaram too has started having conversations with her, especially when his mother is not around. Things look bright for once in Jaya's life until one day Tukaram falls ill. He is coughing continuously and has a high fever. Jaya wants to take him to the local doctor, but the family insists on following the instructions given by their family Guru in treating him. The Guru mandates that they perform religious rituals to help him recover. The family follows his guidance, but Tukaram's health deteriorates, and he starts coughing up blood. Jaya insists on taking him to the city hospital and even requests them to speak to Mangesh.

Her mother-in-law authoritatively declares, "Our family Guru has been treating him, and he has been recovering well, so you don't teach me what has to be done, understand? You keep following my instructions and take care of your husband like a dutiful wife." Jaya is confused and feels helpless, and she spends all her time taking care of her ailing husband. Seeing her dedication, Tukaram confesses, "I'm very sorry Jaya, but we should have informed your family before. I am a TB (tuberculosis) patient, but my mother wanted to keep this under wraps, and she believes that everything will be fine with the blessing of our Guru." Jaya is devastated hearing this; she feels cheated but now has no option left. She suggests to her husband that she can arrange to take him to the city hospital. He denies the offer saying he doesn't want to go against his mother's wishes.

She continues to serve and take care of him and listen to the taunts of her mother-in-law, who blames her for Tukaram's illness. She feels it is Jaya's bad karma that has affected her son, as he was doing well before marriage. She is not aware that Tukaram has confessed the truth to Jaya; she claims that after he got married and Jaya stepped into their house, the illness has engulfed her son. In no time, Tukaram passes away, and Jaya is bombarded with allegations of bringing a bad omen to the house and is packed off to her parent's place. Her mother-in-law is not willing to conduct her son's final rituals at the village crematorium run by Baba. To express her resentment, she plans to travel three to four hours away from Kurni for cremation.

Seeing Jaya return home, *Aai's* world comes crashing down; she is crying uncontrollably, not because of Jaya's loss but because her young widowed daughter is back home in less than six months of being married. If having an unmarried girl at home is considered undesirable, having your widowed daughter back home is considered a curse and taboo in the village. Baba is shocked beyond words, "Madhav, now you know why I told you not to fix this alliance. Look at what has happened," he screams. Madhav angrily retorts, "It's your daughter's fate. Why are you blaming me for everything? How are you sure that if she had married anyone else, she would have not landed back here? Now think of how we are going to manage going forward. The villagers have already started speaking ill about her." He leaves the house furiously; *Aai* is brooding and Baba sits silently looking at Jaya.

Jaya is impassive, with a deadpan expression on her face, unable to comprehend whatever is happening. In a span of a few months, her life has changed drastically – from being a daughter to being a wife and now a widow. Her fate is similar to that of a bird who dreamt of flying freely in the big blue sky until she got caged, but now she is a broken-winged bird who cannot fly. Her circumstances have caged her for life!

GO UP IN SMOKE

*J*aya's return has made the home environment grim. Baba keeps to himself, *Aai* is continuously brooding, and Jaya is silent and sad. Madhav is always in an irritable mood, not wanting to give straight answers to anyone. His body language and mannerisms display his frustration because his hopes of living a city life have dwindled with Jaya's return. Madhav tries to convince Mangesh for the job, but now he tells Madhav that their deal is called off because of Tukaram's death. He asks Madhav to connect with him only if he can arrange enough money to enable him to get the job in the city.

Madhav's behaviour and tone have completely changed; he feels his family is dependent on him, and he is stuck working at the crematorium, which he dislikes. He spits venom when he speaks, especially when he is addressing Jaya, "You are unlucky not only for Tukaram, but also for us; that poor man lost his life, and since you are back here, my chances of prospering and having a better life have become bleak," he taunts. Baba tries correcting him, but Madhav has gotten out of hand. He no longer respects Baba and even answers him by reprimanding him. He doesn't listen to *Aai* and does as he wishes.

After continuously cribbing for a few months, a frustrated Madhav takes to drinking and smoking heavily in front of his parents. He shows his true colours by demanding money from Baba time and again. He declares that if he has to work at the crematorium, he needs to be paid the full amount and be given his liquor supply because no sane guy can handle bodies day in and day out; intoxication is the only solution.

Baba tries reasoning out with him, saying that he and his forefathers have been doing this job without consuming alcohol and that Madhav's demands are uncalled for. Baba asks Madhav to stop drinking and focus on work, but Madhav has made up his mind. He is not going to succumb to whatever Baba is saying. He announces that if he has to work with bodies, he would prefer to work in the city hospital in the mortuary, a job his friend Mangesh is offering.

Mangesh is his confidant who gives him ideas on how to siphon off money from his parents. He even brainwashes Madhav to convince his father to sell the crematorium land, which will fetch them good money, and they all can settle well in the city. Madhav falls into a trap and decides to talk to Baba. When he tells Baba about selling the land, hell breaks loose. For the first time, Baba raises his hand to slap Madhav, but he grabs Baba's hand and says, "Don't try this, Baba, don't try to mess with me; you will have to face the repercussions, and that will be worse than a slap."

He walks out of the house shouting abuses at his parents and sister, blaming them for his ruined life. Baba always knew that Madhav believed in give and take; since childhood, he would only help if his favour was returned in cash or kind. Baba was helpless because Madhav was the heir apparent, and Jaya was never considered for doing this job. Baba had a thin ray of hope that Madhav may change one day, but his defiant behaviour now shattered whatever little hopes he had. Jaya is unable to comprehend Madhav's behaviour and feels terrible about his disrespectful conversation with Baba. *Aai* has an emotional breakdown as she cannot accept whatever has transpired between her husband and son; she is upset. Seeing *Aai*-Baba in this condition,

Jaya is unable to control her emotions. The pair of sobbing women try consoling each other.

Madhav doesn't return home for two days and *Aai* is worried but is scared to ask Baba to enquire about his whereabouts. He returns after two days in a miserable condition. Baba turns away and doesn't give him a second look. Madhav has an emotional breakdown before the most vulnerable person, the only one who believes him and has a soft corner for him – **Aai**. *"Aai,* do you know why I'm looking so lost? Because I got drunk. Don't get me wrong *Aai,* but I drank because I regret whatever I did. I accept the fact that I misbehaved with Baba. I can't face anyone in this world; I'd rather die and let all of you live in peace." He falls at Baba's feet and cries, "I'm very sorry for my behaviour; you can kill me if you want or throw me out of this house. I have wronged you, Baba, please forgive me one last time."

Aai thinks sense has prevailed, and she tries consoling him. She requests Baba to give him one last chance; after all, he is their only hope, their only son. Baba has a passive look and doesn't succumb to whatever Madhav is saying. But an emotional *Aai* coaxes him to believe their son for once. Baba nods his head, uninterested. *Aai* is delighted and believes that the dust has finally settled. His polite behaviour assures her that her son has turned a new leaf. He promises that he will be a devoted son and will diligently work under Baba's guidance.

She asks Jaya to cook Madhav's favourite meal, and she feeds him too. He finishes his dinner and asks his family to sit for dinner, "I will serve all of you with my own hands today," He claims. *Aai* says this is against their tradition and culture, these tasks are assigned to the womenfolk, and no son does them." Madhav comforts her by saying, "Let this be the new beginning of our lives; I want to prove every word I say. I will go the extra mile to do anything to keep my family happy." Jaya and Baba are perplexed by this paradoxical change in Madhav, but *Aai* has tears of joy in her eyes. They all have dinner peacefully and retire to bed.

The next morning a knock on the door awakens Baba. He gets out of bed to open the door; his head is spinning, and he feels drowsy as he walks toward the door. There are a few villagers at the door who want him to perform the funeral formalities. Baba assures to join them soon and help with the rituals. He feels a little lost and looks around the house to find Saku and Jaya still asleep. He can't see Madhav anywhere; he calls out to him but gets no response. Hearing him, both *Aai* and Jaya wake up, looking tired and in a haze.

Before the women can gather their thoughts, Baba blurts out, "He has cheated us once again, Oh! your devoted son. Do you even realise it is 11:00 in the morning, and we are still asleep? Did he want to feed us food? What did he say? Did he want to go the extra mile? He crossed all limits because he fed us some sedatives so that we would get knocked off, or maybe he wanted to kill us. Only he can tell us what his plan was, but now he is not here. He has run away.

I shouldn't have trusted him and let him in this house. We have been cheated by one of our own, now, both of you get up, and from now on, I don't want any discussion about that uncouth Madhav. I have to rush outside and facilitate the funeral rituals; the villagers are waiting for me. One more thing, Madhav is no longer a part of this family, and from today we have severed our ties with him. As I'm helping with the funeral rituals outside, let's believe that these rituals are for Madhav too."

Jaya gets out of bed; her feet are wobbly, but she manages to keep her balance. However, *Aai* is not able to stand on her own; she feels weak at the knees and falls. Jaya helps her up, makes her sit on the bed, and then makes tea to help them get relief from the splitting headache. *Aai* is still in disbelief that Madhav could have wronged them, but she is in for a rude shock when her eyes fall on the open old iron trunk in the corner of the room. She gets up and, with trembling legs, walks towards the trunk; she plonks down on the floor and howls loudly, "he hasn't left anything for us; all the money we saved, whatever little jewellery I had, everything is gone." Jaya rushes to *Aai* to comfort her, but she is gutted this time; she can't stop weeping. Jaya tries convincing her to eat or drink something, but *Aai* has given up; the one she trusted the most has backstabbed her.

By the time Baba is back after completing the funeral formalities, *Aai*'s health has worsened; she is breathing heavily. Baba rushes to the village *Vaidya* (an Ayurvedic medicine practitioner) to get her medicines. By the time he returns *Aai* has fallen asleep, and Jaya is attending to her. "I knew Madhav would never stay true to us, but I never knew he would ditch us and leave us in the lurch. It won't be easy, but I will continue to manage everything, but how will this lady, his mother, ever come to terms with what he has done to us? She has lost faith in humanity. Jaya, you are our only hope; you need to take care of her like a baby; she is your responsibility," sobs Baba. This is the first time Jaya sees a teary-eyed Baba; she holds his hand and assures him that she will do whatever it takes to make *Aai* feel better and take good care of her.

Aai is conscious but bed-ridden, her eyes are always moist, and she keeps remembering Madhav. She is unable to speak to Baba with a straight face and blames herself for giving so much liberty to Madhav. Day in and day out, she keeps apologising to Baba for giving birth to such a worthless son who didn't stand by them and left them at sea. Baba tries to pacify her, but his efforts are ineffective.

Aai's health goes downhill, and after being bed-ridden for three months, she breathes her last. Baba is grief-stricken, hypersensitive to his loss, and numb to the world. For the first time, Jaya is standing next to Baba in the crematorium as he lights his wife's pyre. Jaya, who always wanted to help Baba in the funeral rituals, never knew that her first-hand experience inside the crematorium next to a pyre would be her seeing her mother's death and funeral. She is choked with emotion; she closes her eyes tightly in a vain attempt to hold back her tears. She stands strong like the Rock of Gibraltar, holding Baba as she sees one-half of her life going up in smoke.

SEED OF HOPE

*B*aba sits still like a statue, tears rolling down his eyes non-stop. Jaya is coaxing him to eat something; he has been hungry the whole day. "Why Saku, why did you leave me? What am I supposed to do now? I'm left all alone in this world," he cries. Jaya is short of words; her family has disintegrated in no time, but what hurts her more is that Baba still doesn't consider her as his support system. She feels like a stranger in her own house. Despite her persuading Baba, he refuses to eat and sleeps off on an empty stomach. Jaya too fills her stomach with plain water; she is sleep-deprived and the void in the house haunts her, so she decides to sit outside the hut.

Her mother's pyre has turned to meagre grey ashes. She turns her face and looks upwards at the night sky. She stares blankly, looking for answers to questions she doesn't know. The night is quiet, the sky is cloudy, and the full moon looks pale. Among all the dimly lit stars, she is trying to find one bright star, hoping that Aai will bless her from up there. The unbright illumination in the sky resonates with her dark fate; she feels orphaned and begins to cry. The occasional barking of dogs breaks the silence of the night. She wipes her tears and once again tries star gazing. The shadows from the puffy clouds are taking shape, and she sees a female figure formed in the clouds. "*Aai*, is that you? Can you see me? *Aai*? She questions inquisitively. She stares more intensely and now what she sees is an image of a female warrior with a sword in her hand. Seeing the cloudy image, she jogs her memory and recalls her narration of *"Khoob ladi mardani woh to Jhansi wali Rani thi."* (Fought gallantly, she was the Queen of Jhansi).

She hurriedly enters the hut, ransacks her bag, pulls out the book, and rushes out. The image on the book's cover resembles the cloudy image formed in the sky. She has tears in her eyes, tears of joy this time. The circumstances she faced and her inability to listen to her heart over the last few years made her powerless, but the image in the sky prompts her to re-discover her strength. It feels like a message from the Almighty.

The next day onwards, she takes charge of the house. Baba wakes up and sees the house is spic and span. A picture of *Aai* with a garland around it adorns the wall. He is speechless. Jaya looks at him and gives him a bright smile, "Baba, get up; you need to get fresh, have your tea and breakfast. Do you think *Aai* will be happy seeing you like this?" She asks. Baba nods his head in disapproval; he gets up slowly and follows every instruction given by Jaya. After he gets fresh, he sits to have tea and breakfast. "I don't feel like eating, Jaya; look how our world has turned upside down. What is left for me here?" he asks sadly.

"Baba, you have seen death and bereaved families closely. One day life will end for all of us, but love won't. Death is not the opposite of life; it is a part of life, and we have to accept it. We will continue to live with her memories. Do you think *Aai* will be at peace seeing you in this miserable condition? No, she won't, so you have to pick yourself up and start living again, live for yourself, focus on your job of serving the dead, and ensure that their last journey is peaceful; no one can snatch this fulfilment from you." expresses Jaya.

Baba is in disbelief hearing her, "Jaya, you spoke like a *Gyaani* (a learned person), giving *Pravachan* (discourse); where did you learn all this from? I suddenly feel belittled in front of you," he responds. "No Baba, I am no *Gyaani*, but all this is a part of life; the sooner we accept it, we will be at peace," she says with a warm smile on her face. "God bless you, my child; your words have infused strength in me. I will not cry anymore; I will take each day as it comes and dedicate myself to my job. I never valued you Jaya, but I feel blessed to have you in these trying times. Thank you, *Beta*." Saying this, Baba hugs her and cries.

She is overwhelmed hearing Baba and has never heard such kind words from anyone in her household ever. She believes that even though she is exhausted by whatever has happened, her patience and resilience have helped her sail through and see the light at the end of the dark tunnel.

Time is fleeting. Jaya is managing the house very well; Baba also gives her a free hand in taking stock of the materials needed for the funeral rituals, and she keeps an account of everything related to funeral activities. Baba still has his reservations about involving her in the funeral rituals, but she knows everything at the back of her hand.

Baba is aging, and she requests that he hire someone to assist him at the crematorium. Baba keeps a word with the village *Panchayat* asking them to recommend someone to help him but in vain. Finally, after requesting for a couple of months, Bhola is sent by the *Panch* to the crematorium. Bhola is a 15-year-old orphan who does odd jobs in the village as instructed by the *Panch*. He has qualms about working in the crematorium but is at the mercy of the village *Panchayat* for his livelihood, so he agrees half-heartedly. Bhola joins the crematorium but detests doing anything; he stands afar and waits for Baba to instruct. Jaya observes him and realises that he is not keen on learning or being proactive about anything, and he tries to avoid extra work.

She is unhappy with him being Baba's assistant, as Baba is overworked and tired. She tries driving some sense into Bhola, who has a poker face most of the time, with no response. Baba asks her to maintain her cool, "he is the only one I have got after making many requests to the *Panchayat*; if he leaves, then I will have no one to help me" says Baba. "But Baba, he is not helping you at all; he just stands there waiting for you to instruct; there are certain basic activities he can do even without instructions, but no, he won't; he is very lazy. Instead of asking the *Panchayat* to assign you a helper, you should make a requisition or appeal to them saying that I am capable enough to handle everything in the crematorium and permit me to assist you," she argues. "Jaya, you are out of your senses; I have said this before too. I don't want to disappoint anyone in this village, I am indebted to them for everything. Why don't you understand?" he replies.

"But Baba, the world is changing fast; why don't you at least try putting this across to the *Panchayat*? Maybe they will hear you." She requests. "Jaya, I don't want to be instrumental in introducing any radical changes in this village and not now, at the end of my life. I want the villagers to remember me as a dedicated person who never broke any rules, end of discussion." He sums up. Jaya doesn't argue anymore and goes about doing her work. Baba continues toiling in the crematorium, single-handedly managing every detail with little help from Bhola. Baba is mentally strong, but his body is aging physically, his skin is wrinkled, and he looks paler than before. His walk is unsteady, and he has a limp. He is weaker than he used to be. He has developed a respiratory disease because of continuously facing smoke for many years from the pyres. Jaya ensures he gets treated well by the village doctor, but his condition doesn't improve much. He frequently feels short of breath and has trouble inhaling or exhaling. The doctor advises Baba to go slow on his activities and take ample rest.

One day while Baba is arranging things for a funeral, he faints. Bhola comes to call Jaya. She rushes towards Baba and finds him surrounded by a few villagers. Baba is unconscious, and she asks Bhola to get water immediately. After sprinkling some water on his face, Baba regains consciousness. He tries to get up slowly, but he wobbles and falls again. A few villagers pick him up and reach him to the hut. The clock is ticking and the family that has come for the funeral wants the rites to get done before sunset.

Baba is resting inside the hut; Jaya is attending to him. The villagers send a message to Bhola asking Baba to resume the funeral activity. Jaya is slightly irritated and wants Baba to take some more rest, but he gets up slowly and walks to the door, but the weakness in his legs makes him stumble. He is plagued with fatigue and dizziness; he cannot stand on his feet and sits down at the door of the hut. Jaya gets worried, "Baba you please come in and lie down, everything else can wait." Baba feels helpless and wants to say something but is breathless. Jaya holds him, takes him inside the hut, and asks him to rest. The villagers are whispering to each other as they are perplexed and unaware of how the final rites will happen.

Jaya walks toward the villagers and starts picking up the logs and preps everything that is needed for the final rites. The villagers are stunned and the chatter of their voices starts getting louder. One of the family members comes forward, "What happened? Will your Baba not be helping with the rituals?" he asks. "Baba is unable to stand on his feet; it will be difficult for him to help today. I am his daughter Jaya, and I can help with the rituals."

He immediately snaps, "But how can you do this? You are a woman, and women are not allowed inside the crematorium; forget helping with the rituals. This is against our culture and traditions. What do you all have to say about this?" he asks. There is an uproar; all the villagers are completely against Jaya helping with the rituals. The villagers keep discussing without arriving at any decision when one of them suggests that they need to talk to the *Panch*.

In some time, two members from the *Panchayat* along with the *Sarpanch* (head of a village) arrive at the crematorium. The *Sarpanch* is around 60 years old and is fit and fair with a thick grey moustache.

He wears a pure white cotton dhoti paired with a full-sleeved, crisp shirt, with a bright turban adorning his head. His personality radiates an aura of power and confidence. Jaya finds his face very familiar, but cannot recollect where she has met him before. The *Sarpanch* meets Baba, who is resting in the hut. Realising that Baba will not be in a position to help them, he comes out and announces, "My dear people, given the current situation, it is difficult to get the rites done here, hence we need to make a conscious decision of what needs to be done. We can go to the nearest village and conduct the last rites; it will take us a minimum of three to four hours to reach there, and it is close to sunset now, so I don't know how we all are going to make this happen."

Before anyone can say anything Jaya interrupts, "*Sarpanchji, Namaskar.* You are Mr. Satwalekar, right? I am Jaya. I don't know if you remember me... You visited the village school when I was a student, many years ago. At that time, you were one of the *Panch*. I am the same girl whom you appreciated when I narrated the *Jhansi ki Rani* poem. I am happy to see that you are the Sarpanch today." He smiles, acknowledges her, and continues his discussion with the villagers.

She again interrupts, "*Sarpanchji*, if you don't mind can I ask you something?" He asks all the villagers to keep quiet and listen to what she says. "I am slightly confused and have a question for all of you. If an actor's son or daughter can become an actor, a teacher's kid grows up to become a teacher, and a doctor's daughter can become a doctor, then why can't I take charge of my father's work?" Questions Jaya.

Before she can say anything more, one of the villagers yells angrily, "You girl, whoever you are. Have you gone mad, and how can you talk to our *Sarpanch* like this and ask him such weird questions? Don't you understand we are God-fearing people and don't want to do anything absurd to shake the peace and harmony in this village? Do you understand that women are not encouraged to do all this work?"

"I do understand and respect each one of you. But if you question what women should do and shouldn't, why does everyone praise Jhansi ki Rani for her valour. You all must have heard of Ahilyabai Holkar; she is regarded as one of the finest female rulers in Indian history; if at that time anyone would say women cannot rule, then how would she have set an example for being a Maratha queen who fought the British. Take the example of Savitribai Phule; she was a pioneer in providing education for girls. She became the first female teacher in India, opened a school for girls, and the one who supported her was her husband, Jyotirao Phule. There are many more examples of women who became change makers. Had all these women kept quiet, we would still have been slaves to some foreign ruler. Change is not easy, but change is the only constant. Necessity is the mother of invention, and when I say mother, I mean only a woman can give birth to change in any society," replies Jaya.

The uproar among the villagers increases; they are unable to digest the fact that a woman is asking them all these questions. The *Sarpanch* asks the villager to maintain their cool. "Listen, Jaya; we are trying to sort out things; whatever you are saying is the truth, but whatever you are asking for is not going to be easy for you too, and…"

Before he can finish, Jaya interjects, "If my brother Madhav had been here, then I wouldn't be asking you these questions. Our ancestors have been doing this job, and we are destined to do it generation after generation. Without us, who will get rid of the bodies? Yes, you may appoint someone later, but I'm talking about today. Should we leave this person who is on his last journey to feel orphaned? That is not what has been imbibed in us; we have been taught to respect the dead. Women are considered to be caregivers, so why can't that transform into me giving care to this departed soul? If you still feel what I'm asking for is incorrect, then why doesn't anyone else from the village manage this crematorium? I'm not trying to challenge anyone, but I just want to highlight that my Baba is old and can't do this work anymore; if I don't, then who will?"

The villagers are left pondering over whatever Jaya has spoken. The Sarpanch questions her, "Jaya do you even know what work you will need to do? It is easy for you to ask for all this, but it is a difficult task." Jaya confidently replies, "Yes *Sarpanchji*, this work looks difficult, and no one will want to do it, but deep down, I know that I am doing the most respectful work."

Hearing Jaya, everyone is clear that this courageous woman trusts her instincts and has decided to take the baton in her hands, to take the legacy forward even when she is not sure if she will be understood well and accepted by all. The *Sarpanch* nods his head and realises that what she is speaking makes a lot of sense. He is the first one to approve her name; many others second him. Few villagers express their resentment, to which the *Sarpanch* tells, "If you are not ok with this arrangement, then you can take the responsibility of managing this crematorium or let it run by the family who has been doing it for generations. I think we need to applaud Jaya's mettle; she is a true example of a devoted daughter. She didn't leave us in a lurch, and she has made things easy for us."

All the villagers agree to the decision. Jaya thanks the *Sarpanch* and the villagers with folded hands. She immediately gets going and completes all the funeral formalities like an expert. Baba is lying down in the hut and watching whatever is happening; he is emotional and is teary-eyed seeing his daughter do the work he thought his son would take charge of.

After the rituals are completed and all the villagers leave, the *Sarpanch* comes to Jaya and says, "Now I remember you distinctly. That day too you demonstrated that only a brave warrior who believes in oneself could surpass any hurdle without batting an eyelid. You once again proved that our land can still produce great warriors who can stand up and face any situation single-handedly. I am proud that you belong to this village Jaya. We need to give women an equal place in society. I am happy that you have initiated this change, and I hope this will make our villagers think more progressively. I ensure that I will always support all such initiatives going forward. God bless you."

Jaya feels grateful after hearing the *Sarpanch*; she knows accomplishing this feat was an uphill task for her. From childhood, she dreamt of helping Baba at his work but was always denied her right, and making this happen always looked impossible. But today, whatever happened made her believe that if one has faith and works sincerely towards anything, it will be achieved. The seeds of hope she had sown in her childhood bore fruits today; she looked up at the sky, closed her eyes, and said a small prayer, thanking the Almighty for everything.

RESTFULNESS

*T*oday Baba feels proud of having a daughter like Jaya; he is unable to express himself. He wants to speak so much but feels tongue-tied. Jaya goes up to him and asks, "Did I do the right thing, Baba?" He gets emotional, "I always thought Madhav would be the flag bearer, and he will take this legacy forward. Whenever you spoke to me about giving me a helping hand, I shunned you. I always thought you were a weakling; after all, you are a girl, a vulnerable girl! I never wanted to bring any change to this patriarchal society. I made a big mistake, my child; I'm sorry," cries Baba.

Jaya holds him, "No, Baba, please don't say sorry; everything has a destined time. I am happy that you are proud of me today. Madhav never wanted to do this; forgive him so that his thoughts don't hurt you anymore," she expresses. "You are right, Jaya; maybe Madhav leaving us was destined and a blessing in disguise. Else I would not have realised your true value and potential!" he exclaims. "Now that you believe in me and I have the support of the *Sarpanch* and the villagers, I assure you that I will continue to be dedicated to my work and take our legacy forward. I will serve the dead till my last breath", assures Jaya. Baba blesses her, looks at Saku's photo, and says, "You would have been proud of her today. She is soft-hearted, but rock-solid at her core; she is cool as a breeze but fierce as fire. She has proved that she can embody both sides and face any situation fearlessly. I don't have to worry about anything now."

The peace of the house was restored that night. After months of suffering, there is a sense of accomplishment, and Baba drifts into a carefree sleep, sleeping like a baby. Jaya is tossing and turning; excitement and anxiety don't let her sleep. She knows she has a tough job at hand, but she is confident that she will be able to make a mark. She remembers her teacher; then, she picks up the book and reads through the poem *"Khoob ladi mardani woh to Jhansi wali Rani thi."* (Fought gallantly, she was the Queen of Jhansi); she feels a sense of pride because today a simple village girl like her did something unconventional.

It is now close to a year that Jaya manages the crematorium on her own. Baba guides her, but she has taken charge completely. Even Bhola has become efficient and takes orders well from her. Her devotion to the job and how she handles everything makes one believe that she is very proficient and has years of experience behind her, whereas the truth is only known to Baba and her. The little girl who keenly observed Baba from a distance had absorbed and registered every action of his with great detail. She didn't need any formal training to do the job meticulously.

The villagers are surprised to see Jaya working tirelessly. What fascinates them is the sight of how she does her job with passion, taking extra care of the bodies. She believes that everyone's last journey has to be memorable. She uses her bare hands to work and delicately handles the bodies of accident or burn victims. She takes special care in winter and rubs *ghee* on the palms and legs of the deceased so that there is no problem in lighting the pyre. Baba notices that the deceased's family members feel a sense of gratification when Jaya performs the rituals. Now even the villagers admire Jaya and her caregiving attitude to the deceased person.

Jaya even brings about a change in how the crematorium is run, and the stocks of all the materials are maintained. Instead of Baba going to the market and stocking the material, she negotiates with the material supplier and allocates space for him at the crematorium entrance. He stocks the firewood, *ghee*, incense sticks, flowers, and other materials needed for cremation in this allocated space. The villagers purchase whatever they need from this shop and provide it to Jaya to complete the rituals. The shanty in which Baba used to earlier stock the materials is now a clean space, which Jaya has assigned to Bhola. She has taken him under her wing; he feels indebted to her and does more than what is required. He refers to her as Jaya *Tai (older sister in Marathi)*. After all, for the first time, an orphan like him has a space of his own to call his home, thanks to Jaya.

The *Panchayat* is impressed seeing Jaya run the crematorium seamlessly and appreciates the caring services provided by her. She also proposes to them to support her in making this a respectable profession by allocating more assistants whom she can train so that they can continue managing this place for years to come. The *Sarpanch* once again admires Jaya's zeal for initiating change, and her never give up attitude.

Life couldn't be better for Baba and Jaya. Baba is doing well health-wise too. Jaya not only trains Bhola on the rituals to be conducted at the crematorium but also teaches him to read and write. The peace and calm at the crematorium signals restfulness – the restfulness of Jaya, who runs the crematorium, and the restfulness of those whose last journey culminates here!

OVERWHELMED

*L*ife and work are normal for Jaya at the crematorium. One day a silent crowd enters the crematorium. The *Sarpanch*, Mr. Satwalekar, leads the funeral. He looks distraught; he is in a white dhoti, bare-chested with a *Janeu (the sacred thread worn primarily by Brahmins)*, and his head is uncovered, displaying his bald pate. He is carrying a pot containing the ignited fire in his right hand. One of the villagers informs Jaya that the *Sarpanch's* older sister has passed away, and she needs to get things ready for the cremation. Jaya and Bhola quickly start doing whatever is required. The *Sarpanch* wants sandalwood logs for his sister's pyre, a rare demand in a small village. Unfortunately, the shop at the crematorium entrance doesn't stock sandalwood, so the shopkeeper assures us to arrange the same as soon as possible. The mourners are waiting at the crematorium. Jaya has arranged everything required to do the last rites; only the sandalwood logs are awaited.

Everyone's attention is suddenly diverted to a 30-year-old woman who comes into the crematorium. She is sobbing and says, "*Mamaji*, please let me do the needful." The *Sarpanch* turns a deaf ear. She is pleading with him; everyone is looking at her, some villagers rolling their eyes and exchanging looks out of confusion. The villagers are speaking in whispers so the *Sarpanch* wouldn't hear them. She continues sobbing, "Please, *Mamaji,* let me see my mother's face. You had promised me in my childhood you would fulfil all my wishes. Don't turn your back on me." Before the *Sarpanch* could react, one villager shouts, "You girl, who are you, who let you in? Don't you know that women are not allowed inside the crematorium; leave now." "But that is my mother, I want to be with her, I will never get to see her ever again," she bawls.

Few more villagers revolt, "Leave the crematorium; you are not allowed here." One young villager pushes her. Jaya, who is looking at the commotion from afar, comes running and picks the woman. The older men start taunting, "Go away from here. You are a woman; you are not supposed to enter the crematorium." Jaya turns around and says, "Should I also leave from here? I am a woman too!" The villagers keep quiet, the *Sarpanch* asks Jaya not to interfere in his family matters. Jaya doesn't say anything; she asks the woman to sit and offers her some water to drink, which she refuses.

"If you don't mind, can I ask you what happened?" asks Jaya. In between sobs, the woman replies, "I am Roshni and it's my mother's funeral. The *Sarpanch* of this village is my *Mamaji (mother's brother)*. Since childhood, he always supported me and encouraged me to do whatever I liked. My father abandoned my mother and me when I was a child. *Mamaji* was the true pillar of support for the two of us. He was instrumental in educating me and ensuring that I followed my dreams and became a journalist. But things went downhill when I secretly married my colleague, Akram. I was scared that my family might not accept him, so I thought if I married him and then told them, they would give their consent. But I was wrong. *Mamaji* broke all ties with me; he even asked my mother to sever ties with me. But my mother kept in touch with me without his knowledge. She wanted all of us to stay together as one happy family, but alas." Jaya strokes her head and tries to pacify her.

In some time, the sandalwood is brought to the crematorium. Jaya gets up to start the final rituals.

Roshni says, "I know everyone believes in traditions, and no one wants to break any rule out of fear, but I always wanted to light my mother's pyre. That was her last wish too. But I know all these people staring at me can't stand my sight in the crematorium; how will they let me fulfil my wish." She clutches Jaya's hands, her eyes expressing hopelessness, "Can you speak to my *Mamaji*, requesting him to let me fulfil my wish?" Jaya nods her head and goes to *Sarpanchji*.

"*Sarpanchji*, I'm nobody to say anything, but I know you have a large heart. Can I make a small request? Please let Roshni light her mother's pyre; she is feeling miserable, and she is sorry for whatever happened in the past. But if you let her light the pyre, she will not only fulfil her mother's wish but also consider this as a closure, and let her pay her last respects to her mother in the desired manner. Please, *Sarpanchji*, please." *Sarpanchji* gets angry on hearing Jaya's request. He disagrees and says that he will not let Roshni do the last rites and threatens to walk out of the crematorium. Jaya stops him and expresses, "*Sarpanchji*, you were the only one standing in my support when I wanted to take charge of my father's work at this crematorium. You spoke so positively and brought about a change. You told everyone that both son and daughter are equal, so why shouldn't Roshni light her mother's pyre? Is it her mother's fault that she didn't have a son? If someone doesn't have a son, why can't their daughter perform the required rituals? The love and respect one has for their parents doesn't change, be it a daughter or a son. You should be proud of your niece; she is only asking for what is due to her and what is her right; every daughter is liable to perform her parent's last rites."

"Jaya, you don't know what you are talking about. Performing the last rites of parents is the responsibility of a son or any other male member of the family. So don't debate with me on this and let me do the needful." He retorts. *"Sarpanchji*, you are very well aware that women are breaking stereotypes and shattering the age-old patriarchal beliefs; one example is standing in front of you. There have been many cases where ordinary women too lit their parent's funeral pyre. What would happen if Roshni were to light her mother's pyre? She is also a breathing, living body, engulfed in emotional turmoil. You spoke with so much assurance the other day, saying that you are ready to support women achieve the cause. Why are you shying away today? You have all the right to stay angry with Roshni for the rest of your life, but today she needs your support. Please let her do the needful. Someone needs to reconsider the prevalent gender inequality and clear the patriarchal mental blocks not only in our village but in our country. *Sarpanchji,* everyone respects you, and only you can bring about the change in our village. Please be that agent of change, and every daughter will respect you more for permitting them to do this noble deed. Please, *Sarpanchji*, please," she requests.

Sarpanchji wipes his tears and, with folded hands, announces, "My dear villagers, I'm grateful to all of you for standing by me during these trying times. I have one more request to make. Many of you may think I am a rule-breaker, but all I would say is I am just a change maker. I don't want to deprive anyone of whatever is due to them. Therefore, I will let my niece Roshni light her mother's pyre; this is her duty as she is the only child of my late sister. She is not her son, but she is more than a son to her, so I cannot snatch her off what is due to her." Hearing this, there is a hustle-bustle among the villagers. Roshni runs towards her *Mamaji* and falls at his feet. He picks her up, gives her a tight hug, and calms her. Some villagers leave the crematorium displaying their disagreement about whatever is about to happen.

Baba, who is resting inside the hut, is happy to hear the *Sarpanch's* announcement. He is proud that his daughter Jaya has a role in influencing *Sarpanchji,* and she is instrumental in bringing about one more change in the village.

Sarpanchji looks at Jaya and instructs her to guide Roshni. She willingly holds Roshni's hands and directs her step by step. Both Jaya and Roshni feel gratified. Roshni gives a warm hug to Jaya, thanking her, "You are God sent; without you, I wouldn't have been able to do any of this. I thank you from the bottom of my heart." She expresses herself emotionally. Jaya manages to smile at Roshni, too overwhelmed by her emotions to speak.

CONQUEROR OF DEATH

One by one, the mourners leave the crematorium. Roshni is standing still, watching the pyre burn; bits of ash are flying high and all around. A flood of thoughts raging in her head, and the grief on her face depicts an array of emotions. *Sarpanchji* walks to her, "*Beta*, let's go home; you must be tired." He says with concern. "*Mamaji*, can I wait here for some more time? If you say no, I will leave with you right away." She requests. "Stay on, my child; I know what you are feeling; take your time. I will go home and get everything else ready for the other rituals to be performed in the days to come," he says.

Roshni is standing there; it's been more than an hour, and she is taking her time. It is still not easy for her to accept her mother's loss or rush through the moments of saying goodbye and letting go. Bhola comes to Roshni, pointing towards the hut, he tells her that Jaya *Tai* is asking her to come there. Roshni looks in the direction of the hut; Jaya is signalling her to come to the hut, and Roshni half-heartedly walks towards her. She enters the hut and meets Baba, resting in the corner. Jaya gives her a glass of water. Baba says, "I'm lucky to have Jaya as my daughter; she is the conqueror of death; she is God's special child."

People who come here for the first time are surprised to see a woman doing this job, but my Jaya works with passion. You also must have wondered how a woman is managing this crematorium, right? But my Jaya is extraordinary. Do you know she takes extra care of the bodies because she believes their last journey must be memorable?" There is pride in his voice. Jaya feels embarrassed hearing Baba praising her; she tells him, "Baba take rest; the doctor has asked you not to talk so much. Do you know Baba? She is our *Sarpanchji's* niece; she is a journalist from Mumbai?" Baba hears attentively.

Roshni adds, "My decision to marry Akram changed everything. My mother moved back to her maternal home and started living here with *Mamaji*. My mother has been ailing for the last few months, and she kept requesting I meet her. But I was afraid of *Mamaji*; how would I face him, but finally I gathered the courage to come here. I reached *Mamaji's* house this morning and was shocked to see a huge crowd there. I silently followed the crowd to the crematorium, and whatever happened after that is known to you both."

Jaya gives her tea and some snacks. Roshni holds Jaya's hand and thanks her once again for all the help she rendered. Seeing Jaya's multi-faceted personality, the journalist in Roshni awakens.

"Can I take your interview Jaya?" She asks.

Jaya starts giggling, "Am I any celebrity or politician that you want to interview me Madamji?" replies Jaya.

"I know you are an ordinary person, but do you realise you are doing an extraordinary job—a job, which any man in the world would shudder doing. You have proved Jaya that only a woman can do such an unconventional job and that too with passion!" pat comes Roshni's reply. Jaya is still pondering on what she heard, and before she can say something, Roshni asks, "So how can I start my interview? I would like to record your voice Jaya; I hope you don't mind? Will you have a paper and pen? I would like to jot down a few things." Jaya hands over a pencil and notebook to her. Jaya looks at Baba; he nods his head, giving her an assuring glance signalling her to go ahead with the interview.

"How do you manage to do all this, Jaya, like applying ghee on the feet and palms of the body? asks Roshni. Jaya looks her straight in her eye and replies, "Madamji, I am sure you must be applying cold cream in winters, right? It is the same logic; the body is dead but not the soul. The last journey has to be a pleasant one."

Jaya offers snacks to Roshni, but she is disinterested. "Will you tell me the truth, Jaya? For doing this job in such a sane manner, you must be taking a sip or two, wouldn't you? I hope you are getting what I'm trying to ask. Don't worry, I won't publish this!" winks Roshni. Jaya smirks," Madamji, people drink or get intoxicated to run away from the truth, but there is no greater truth than death." Jaya sips on her tea and munches on the *pakora* (a spiced fritter); she asks Roshni to eat too.

Roshni extends her hand to pick a *pakora* and hesitates. She suddenly realises that Jaya was handling a dead body a while ago, and now, she is offering the snack prepared by the same hands. Roshni is unsure as to how she will eat what Jaya has cooked? She moves her hand back and pops the next question, "Please don't mind me asking but do your family members eat food cooked by you?" Jaya looks at Baba, smiles, and says, "I not only cook but, if need be, feed Baba with my own hands too. Tell me one thing Madamji, in your city, don't the doctors who do high-end operations and surgeries eat with their own hands?" Roshni is spell-bound, because here is a lady giving valid answers without batting an eyelid, and everything she is saying is making sense.

Roshni's hand automatically moves towards the plate, and in no time, she empties the *pakoras*. "Jaya, tell me honestly, don't you ever get scared of these dead bodies?" Jaya nods her head and says, *"Madamji, zinda logon se darr zaroor lagta hain, laashon se kya darna!"* (At times, I fear the people who are alive, why be afraid of these harmless dead bodies!)

Roshni is content with meeting someone so genuine. She gets up and hugs Jaya. She realises it's the warmest hug she has received in ages; it reminds her of her deceased mother. Jaya walks her to the door. Roshni turns around and asks her, "Are you happy doing this job? After all, you are a woman, and we women are mostly looked down upon, especially if we are breaking the norm and doing anything exceptional?"

Jaya replies, "Madamji, this job empowers me. People will look down on me for doing this job as a woman and a widow. But they don't realise that your gender, caste, or marital status does not matter on a cremation ground. I live with that belief and will continue serving the dead. Women and their actions will always be questioned, but change is the only constant, and every norm has the right to change so that we can create new ones to help us progress!"

"I completely agree with you, Jaya; you empowered me to light my mother's pyre today. Most of us assume and never ask our elders for whatever is due to us. But if we ask, many age-old practices, which are blindly followed, can be eradicated, exactly the way you did. People will always express their resentment, but that shouldn't stop us from speaking up. One last question Jaya. If I ask you to describe your life in one sentence, then what would you say?" Jaya answers, "I have made a life, living amongst the dead and a livelihood by serving them!"

Roshni returns to Mumbai after completing the thirteen-day rituals for her mother. She still can't get over her soul-stirring conversation with Jaya. Jaya's approach to life and death inspires Roshni to tell the world about Jaya, an 'Ordinarily Extraordinary

Woman'. She decides to write an article on Jaya's life story. She picks a blank paper and writes in bold capital letters **MrityunJaya**, the one who has conquered death and emerged victoriously!

www.ingramcontent.com/pod-product-compliance
Lightning Source LLC
LaVergne TN
LVHW041627070526
838199LV00052B/3273